Dear Shelley
Merry Christmas
We love you!
Mom & Dad
1988

Brian Thompson

VIKING
FIRST
PICTURE
DICTIONARY

Illustrated by Celia Berridge

VIKING KESTREL

VIKING KESTREL

Published by the Penguin Group
27 Wrights Lane, London W8 5TZ, England
Viking Penguin Inc., 40 West 23rd Street, New York, New York 10010, USA
Penguin Books Australia Ltd, Ringwood, Victoria, Australia
Penguin Books Canada Ltd, 2801 John Street, Markham, Ontario, Canada L3R 1B4
Penguin Books (NZ) Ltd, 182–190 Wairau Road, Auckland 10, New Zealand

Penguin Books Ltd, Registered Offices: Harmondsworth, Middlesex, England

First published in Great Britain by Puffin/Viking Kestrel 1988
and simultaneously in the USA by Viking Kestrel

Filmset in Century Schoolbook (Linotron 202) by
Rowland Phototypesetting Ltd, 30 Oval Road, London NW1 7DE
Printed and bound in Great Britain by
William Clowes Limited, Beccles and London

ISBN 0–670–82154–3

Aa

apple

astronaut

ant

avocado

arrow

Bb

ball

balloon

basket

banana

baby

Bb

black

bear

bicycle

bird

Bb

blue

book

bottle

boat

bridge

Bb

brown

button

bricks

butterfly

Cc

car

cat

camel

caterpillar

camera

Cc

computer

crab

clock

chair

crocodile

Dd

dog

doll

door

dinosaur

Dd

dragon

dress

drum

duck

Ee

eye

egg

elephant

ear

Ff

five

fence

fish

fire

Ff

fly

four

flag

flower

fork

Ff

fruit

fountain

foot

frog

Gg

gate

giraffe

gloves

giant

Gg

goat

goldfish

grapes

green

guitar

Hh

hammer

hat

hamster

hand

Hh

house

hen

helicopter

horse

Ii

ice

iceberg

ink

ice-cream

island

Jj

jug

juggler

jacket

jeans

jigsaw

Kk

kettle

kangaroo

knife

knitting

key

Ll

log

lemon

ladder

lion

leaf

Mm

matches

map

magnet

milk

Mm

moon

monkey

motorcycle

mouse

Nn

nail

needle

nuts

nest

net

nurses

Oo

orange

octopus

one

ostrich

owl

oranges

P p

panda

parrot

paints

parachute

Pp

penguin

pencil

pink

pig

P p

pin

pigeon

piano

puppy

Qq

quail

quilt

queen

Rr

red

radio

rainbow

rabbit

Rr

ruler

robot

ring

rope

rocket

abcdefghijklmn opqr**s** tuvwxy

Ss

saw

scissors

sheep

sand castle

shark

Ss

shirt

ship

shoe

sock

skeleton

Ss

spider

spoon

snowman

snake

snail

Ss

stamp

submarine

swing

star

string

Tt

table

television

telephone

tadpoles

Tt

three

tiger

tent

teddy bear

Tt

tortoise

towel

tomato

toothbrush

Tt

train

tree

tractor

trumpet

two

Uu

underwear

umbrella

unicorn

Vv

vase

volcano

violin

vegetables

Ww

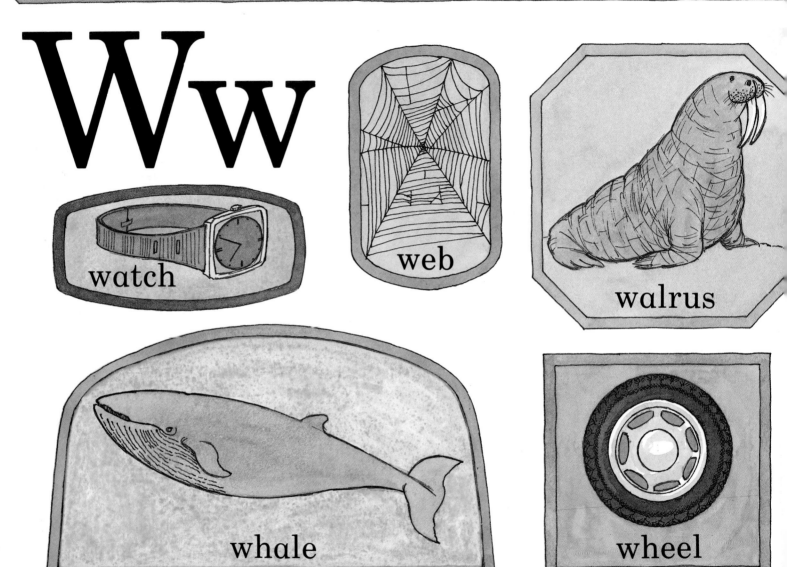

watch

web

walrus

whale

wheel

Ww

worm

witch

windmill

wool

window

Xx

xylophone

x-ray

Yy

yellow

yo-yo

yogurt

yacht

Zz

zig-zag

zip

zebra

ALPHABETICAL WORD LIST

Aa
ant
apple
arrow
astronaut
avocado

Bb
baby
ball
balloon
banana
basket
bear
bicycle
bird
black
blue
boat
book
bottle
bricks
bridge
brown
butterfly
button

Cc
camel
camera
car
cat
caterpillar
chair
clock
computer
crab
crocodile

Dd
dinosaur
dog
doll
door
dragon
dress
drum
duck

Ee
ear
egg
elephant
eye

Ff
fence
fire
fish
five
flag
flower
fly
foot
fountain
frog
fruit

Gg
gate
giant
giraffe
gloves
goat
goldfish

grapes
green
guitar

Hh
hammer
hamster
hand
hat
helicopter
hen
horse
house

Ii
ice
iceberg
ice-cream
ink
island

Jj
jacket
jeans
jigsaw
jug
juggler

Kk
kangaroo
kettle
key
knife
knitting

Ll
ladder
leaf
lemon
lion
log

Mm
magnet
map
matches
milk
monkey
moon
motorcycle
mouse

Nn
nail
needle
nest
net
nurses
nuts

Oo
octopus
one
orange
oranges
ostrich
owl

Pp
paints
panda
parachute
parrot
pencil
penguin
pig
pink

Qq
quail
queen
quilt

Rr
rabbit
radio
rainbow
red
robot
rocket
rope
ring
ruler

Ss
sand castle
saw
scissors
shark
sheep
ship
shirt
shoe

skeleton
sock
snail
snake
snowman
spider
spoon
stamp
star
string
submarine
swing

Tt
table
tadpoles
teddy bear
telephone
television
tent
three
tiger
tomato
toothbrush
tortoise
towel
tractor
train
tree
trumpet
two

Uu
umbrella
underwear
unicorn

Vv
vase
vegetables
violin
volcano

Ww
walrus
watch
web
whale
wheel
windmill
window
witch
wool
worm

Xx
x-ray
xylophone

Yy
yacht
yellow
yogurt
yo-yo

Zz
zebra
zig-zag
zip